I LOVE YOU... ™

Big Book of Stickers

Modern Publishing
A Division of Unisystems, Inc.
New York, New York 10022

Printed in India
Series UPC:11706

I LOVE FALL!

I LOVE THE FOREST!

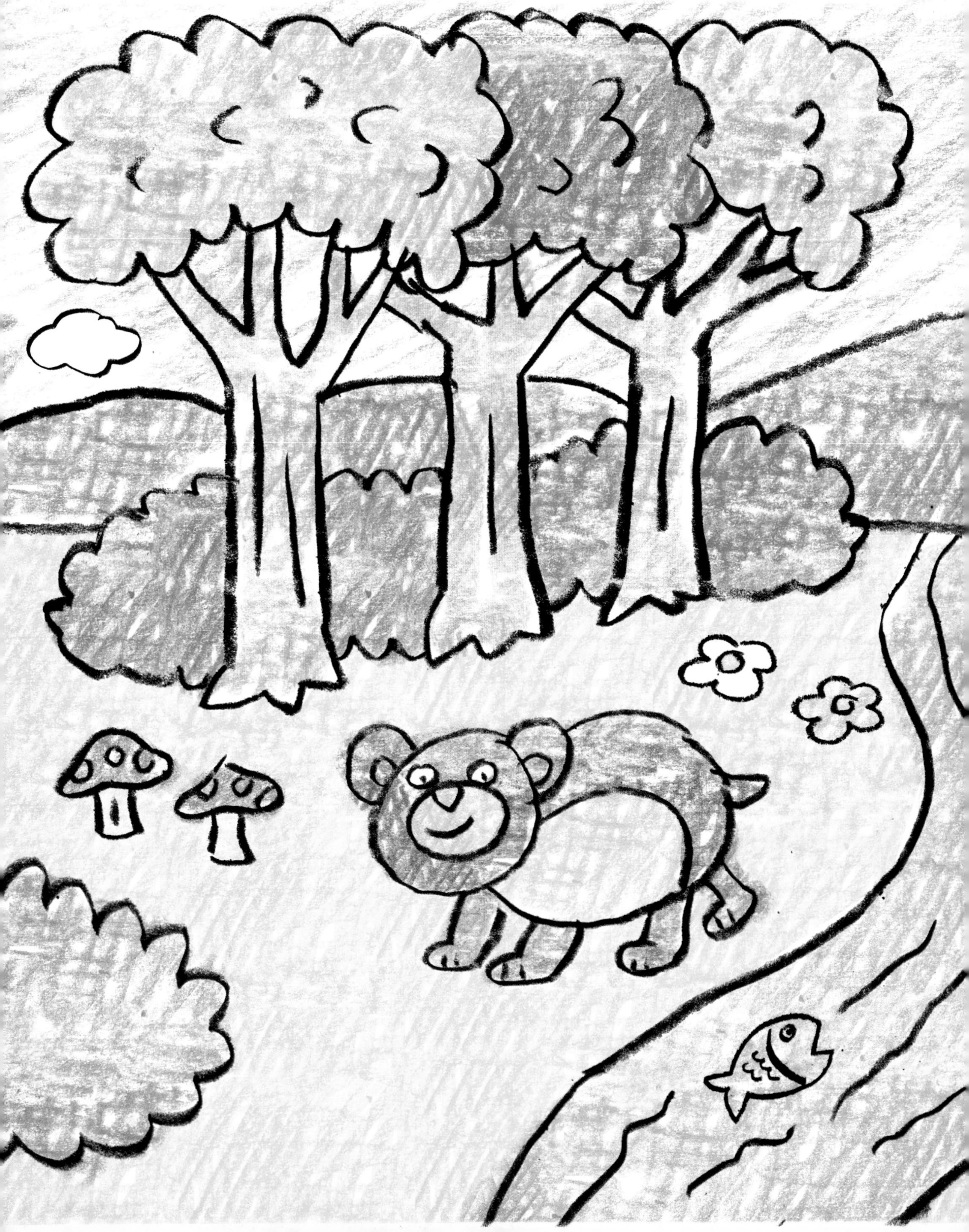

I LOVE MY BACKYARD!

I LOVE DAYTIME!

I LOVE TO HAVE FUN!

I LOVE COOKING!

I LOVE MY BACKYARD!

I LOVE THE BEACH!

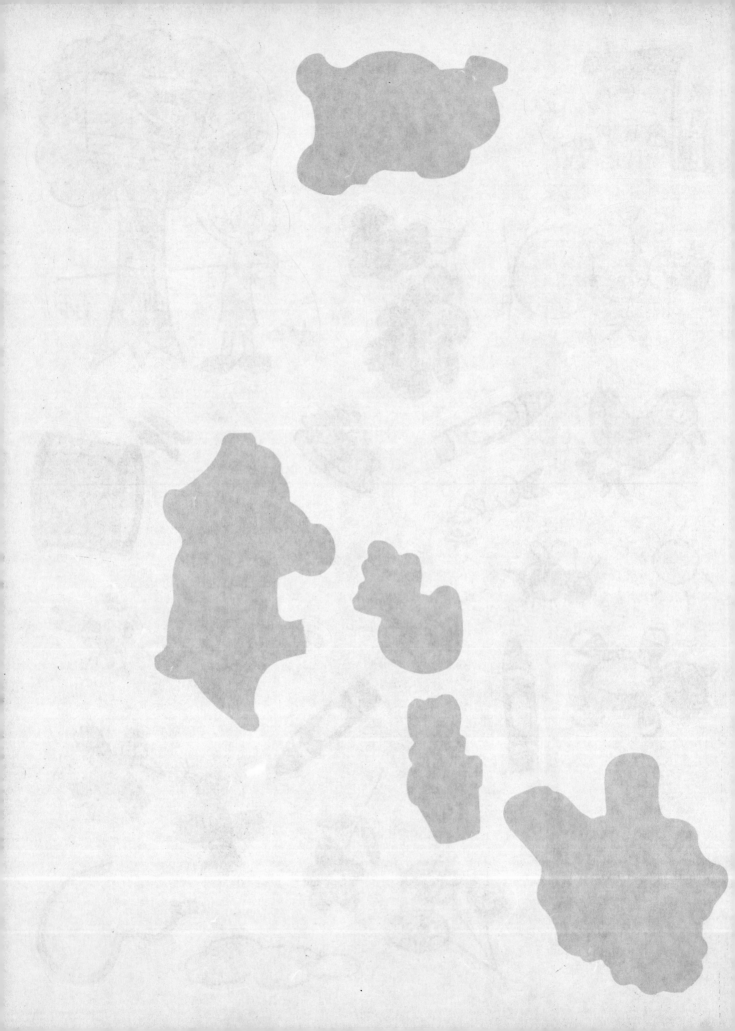

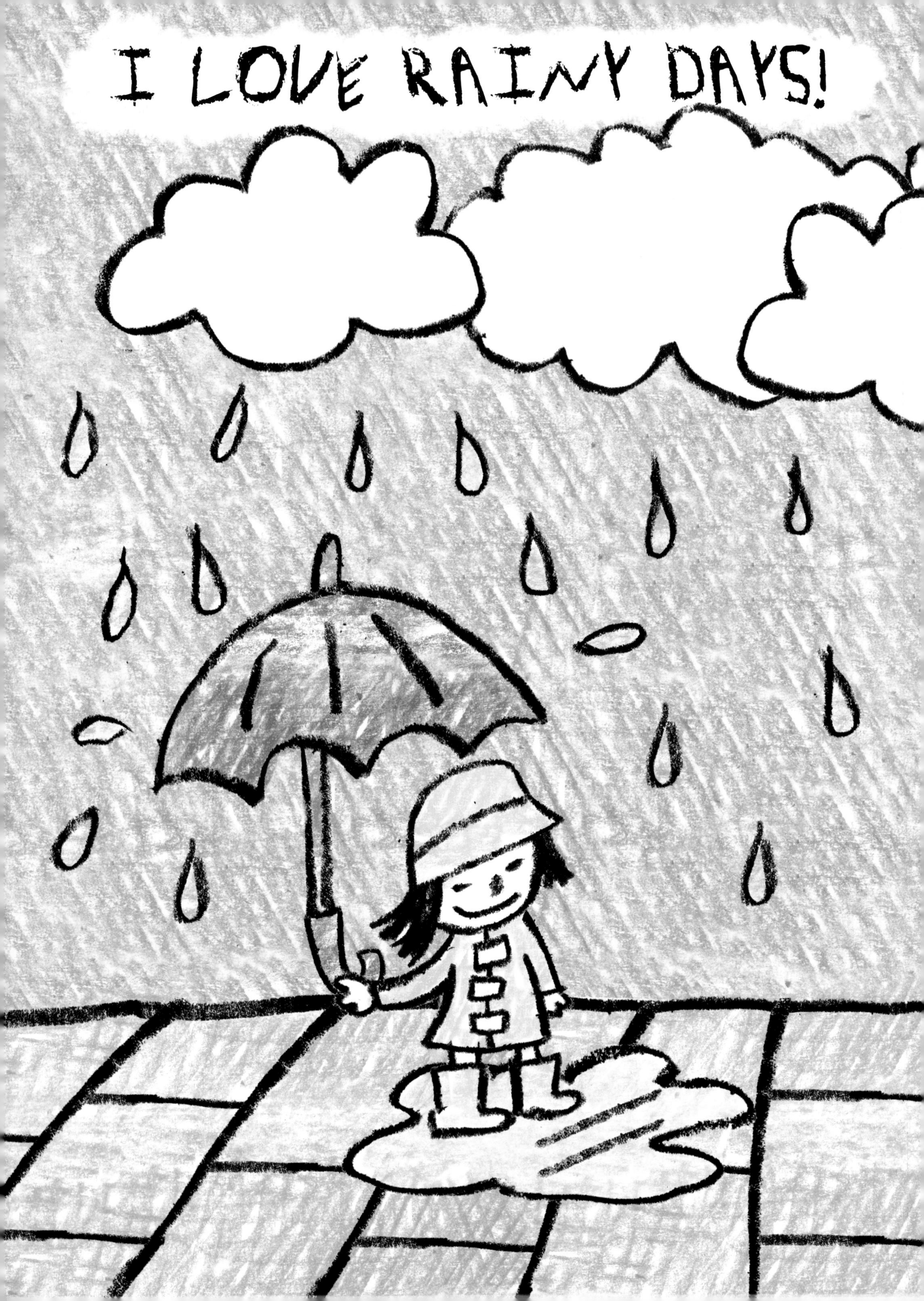
I LOVE RAINY DAYS!

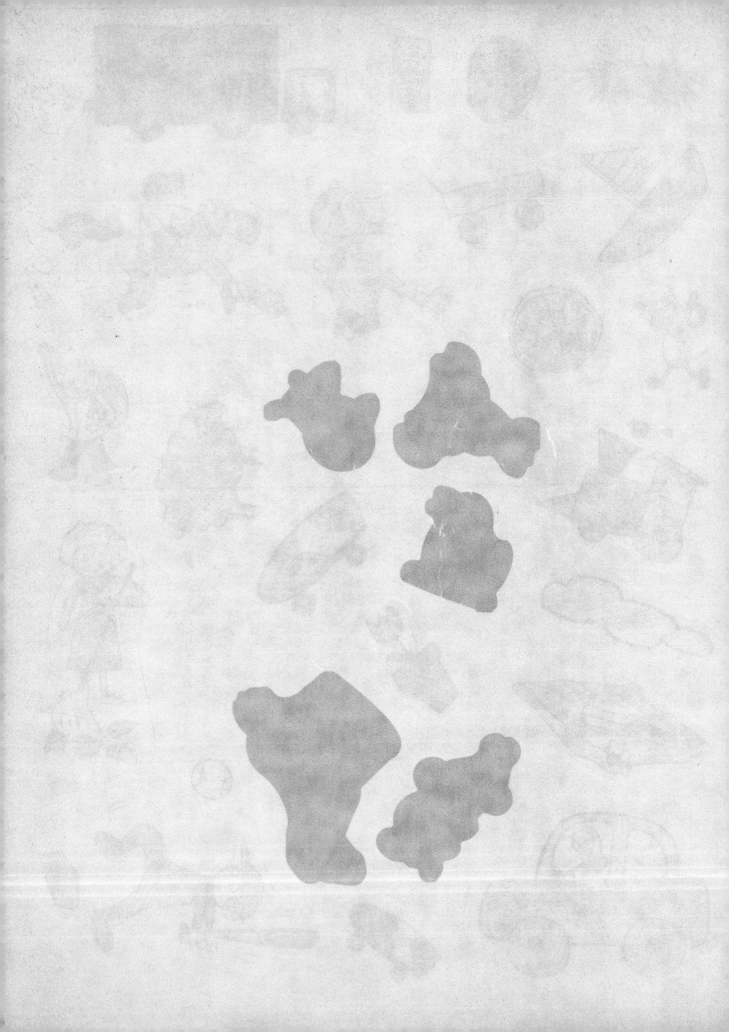

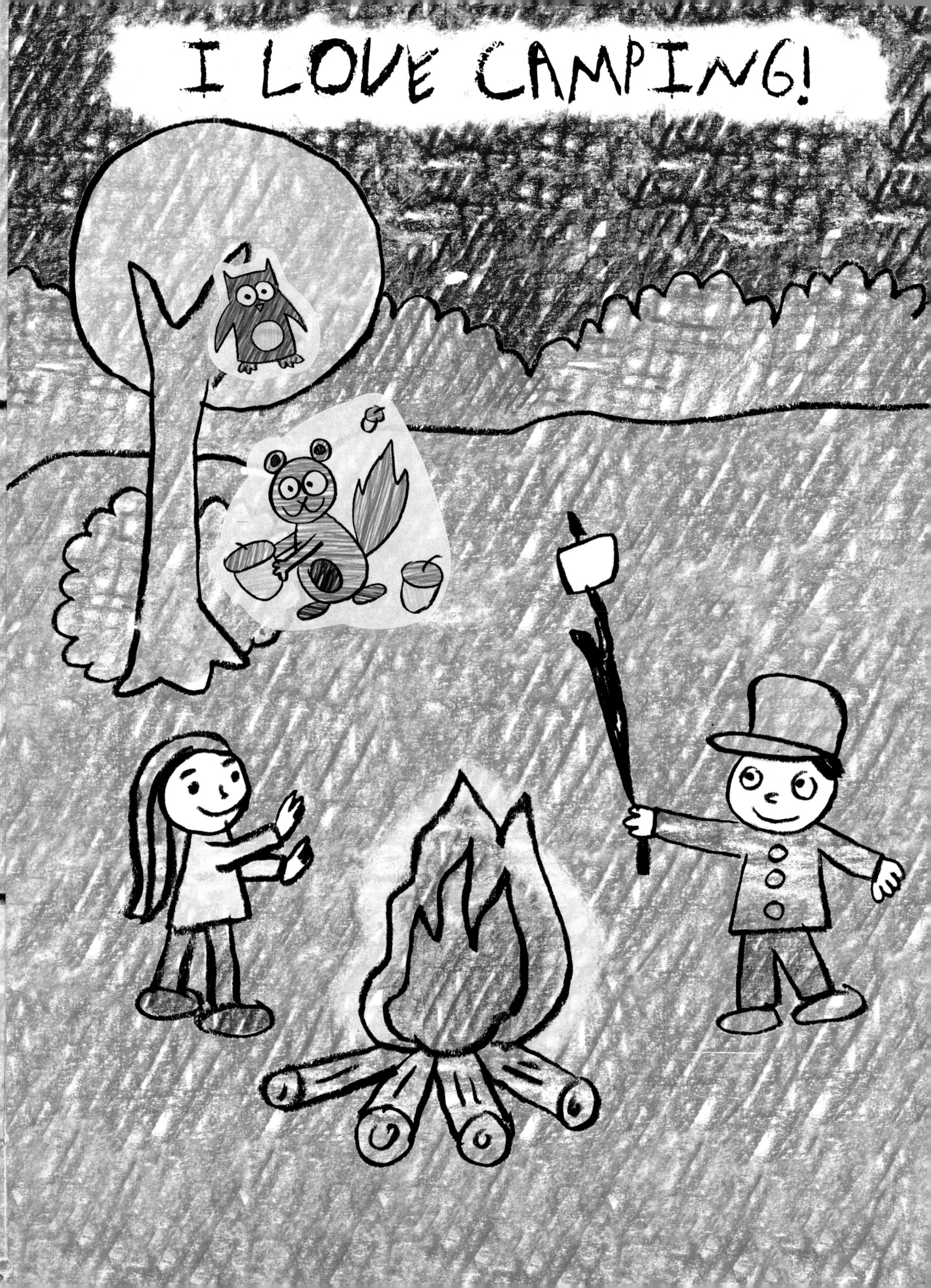
I LOVE CAMPING!

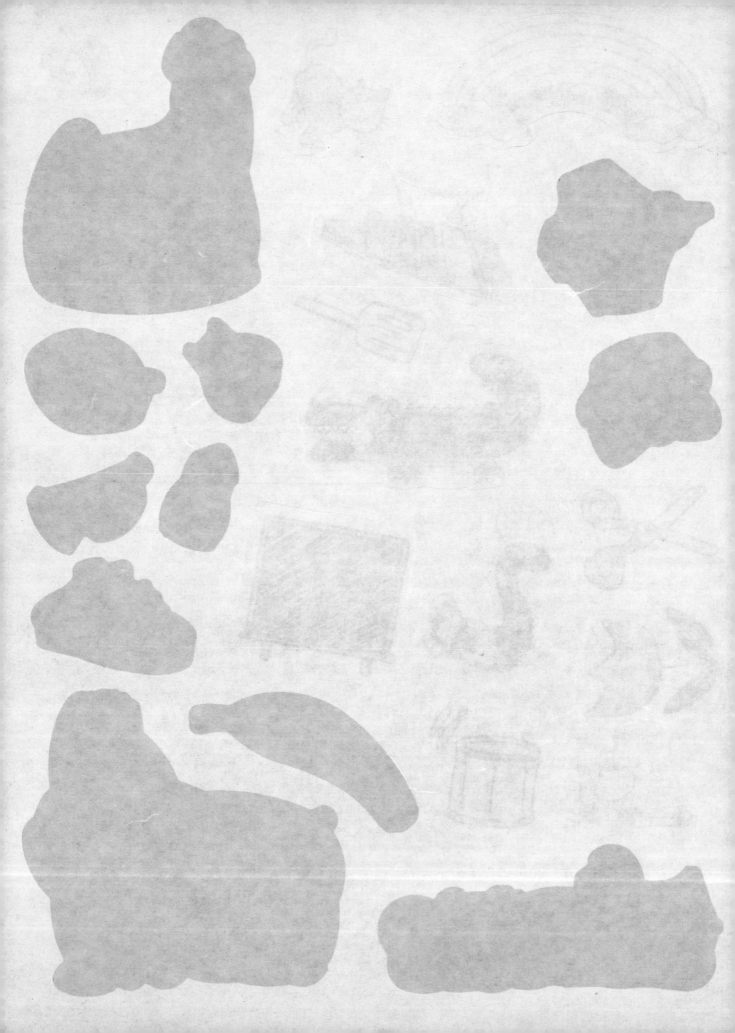

I LOVE THE MUSEUM!

I LOVE DESSERT!

I LOVE THE SKY!

I LOVE CONCERTS!

I LOVE GOING TO THE MOVIES!

I LOVE GARDENING!

I LOVE THE PLAYGROUND!

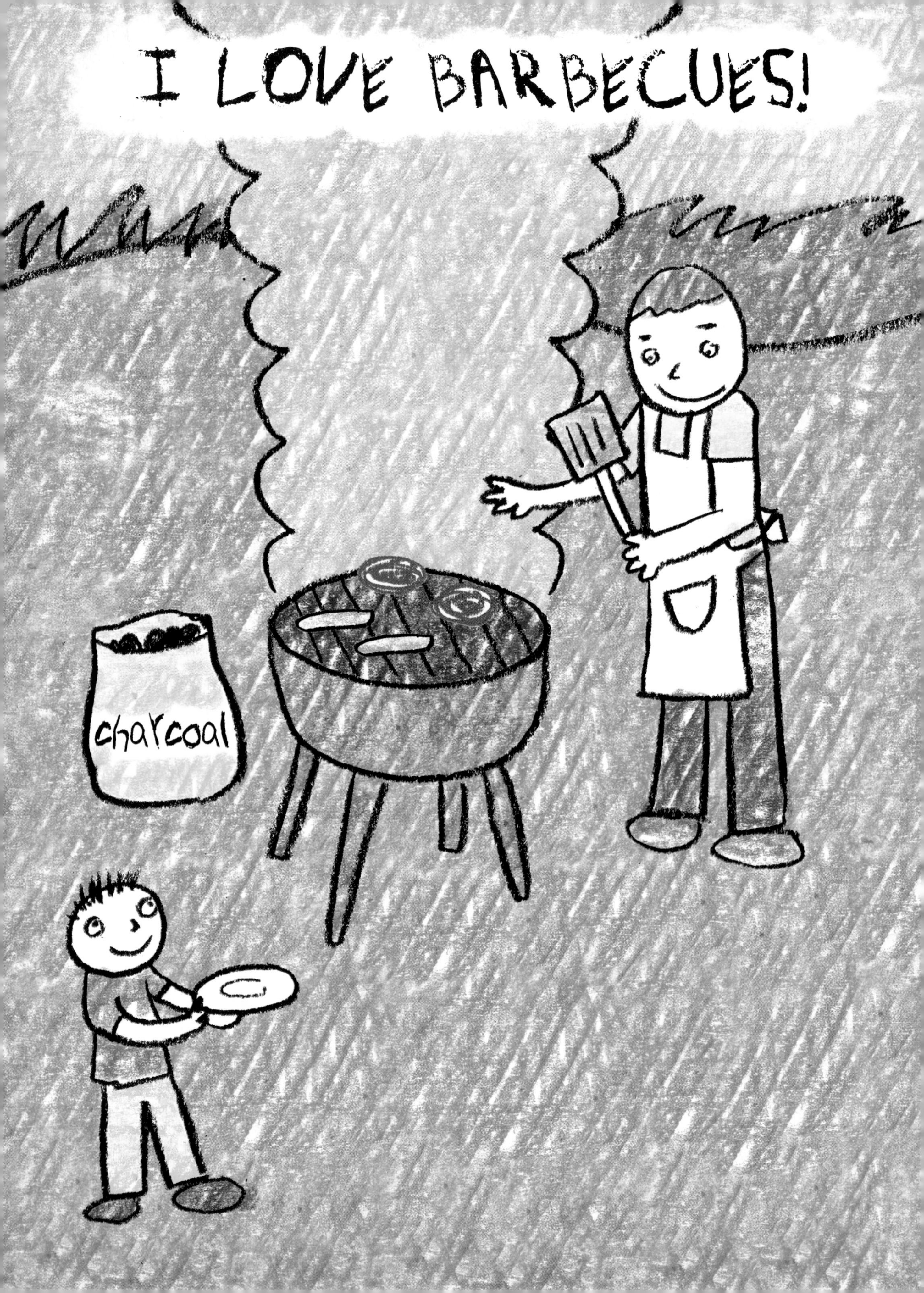
I LOVE BARBECUES!
charcoal

I LOVE SNACK TIME!